Pig Little

Mike Thaler

illustrated by Paige Miglio

Henry Holt and Company · New York

Henry Holt and Company, LLC
Publishers since 1866
175 Fifth Avenue, New York, New York 10010
www.henryholtchildrensbooks.com

Henry Holt® is a registered trademark of Henry Holt and Company, LLC.
Text copyright © 2006 by Mike Thaler
Illustrations copyright © 2006 by Paige Miglio
All rights reserved. Distributed in Canada by H. B. Fenn and Company Ltd.

Library of Congress Cataloging-in-Publication Data
Thaler, Mike.
Pig Little / Mike Thaler ; illustrated by Paige Miglio.—1st ed.
p.   cm.
ISBN-13: 978-0-8050-6977-8 / ISBN-10: 0-8050-6977-1
1. Swine—Juvenile poetry. 2. Family—Juvenile poetry. 3. Beaches—Juvenile poetry.
4. Children's poetry, American. I. Miglio, Paige, ill. II. Title.
PS3570.H3176P54 2006   811'.54—dc22   2005012729

First Edition—2006 / Designed by Donna Mark
Printed in the United States of America on acid-free paper. ∞

10 9 8 7 6 5 4 3 2 1

The artist used watercolor and water-soluble color pencil
to create the illustrations for this book.

In loving memory of Laurel Lee Thaler
—M. T.

To all the beach lovers, young and old,
of Laurel Beach
—P. M.

Leaving

Pig Little's mom was ready to go.
Pig Little's dad was ready to go.
Pig Little's sister was ready to go.
Pig Little was *not* ready to go.
He couldn't find his cap.
He looked behind the dresser.
He looked inside his toy box.
In came his mom.
In came his dad.
In came his sister.
"Why aren't you ready to go?"
they all asked.
"I can't find my cap,"
sniffled Pig Little.
"It's on your head,"
they all said.
Pig Little reached up.
It was there.
He smiled,
then he ran out the door
ahead of them all.

Driving

Pig Little
loved to drive
the car.
He ran it
with his window knob.
When he pushed it forward,
the car went faster.
When he pulled it back,
the car stopped.
He was happy
to sit quietly
and let his mom think
that she was doing
all the driving.

The Beach

Pig Little
loved the beach.
He loved the sand.
There was so much of it.
There was
always enough
to build
a castle
with six towers.
And he loved
the waves.
There were so many
of them.
And whenever
he asked,
one was *always* happy
to splash
his feet.

Clouds

Pig Little
lay on his back
and looked up
in the sky
as:
       fluffy
          elephants
              turned
                  into
                      umbrellas,

cotton camels
      traded
           humps,

a floating clown
     petted
         a cloud lion
           as it opened
              its mouth wide
                in a silent
                  roar.

Lunch

For lunch
Pig Little
ate
a peanut butter
sandwich.
Unfortunately
at the beach
it was more SAND
than
WICH.

The Ice Cream Cone

For dessert
Pig Little
got
an ice cream cone.
He licked it fast,
but the sun
licked it too,
so Pig Little
decided
that they
would just
share it.

The Shovel

Pig Little
had a blue shovel.
He was great
at making
hills,
but whenever he made
a hill
he also made
a hole,
and the taller
he made the hill,
the deeper
he made the hole.
That is why
Pig Little decided
he was great
at making both
hills
and
holes.

The Parade

Pig Little
loved a parade.
He tooted
his trumpet.
He banged
his drum.
He marched along
having lots
of fun.
He didn't even mind that
he was a parade
of one.

Treasure

Pretending
he was a pirate,
Pig Little
strode along the seashore
searching
for buried treasure.
And he found it!
As he carefully
filled his treasure chest
with
pearly shells,
painted rocks,
and polished glass,
he smiled.
"And I don't even have
a pirate map."

Sunset

It was late.
The sun
began to sink
into the ocean.
Pig Little hoped
that all the water
would not
put out
the sun's
fire.

Bye-Bye

Pig Little
didn't want
to go home,
for the beach
was his friend.
It had given him
a day full of memories
and a bucket
full of treasure.
And when he sadly turned
to wave good-bye
to the ocean,
he had to smile,
for the ocean
waved back
at him.

Flying

Pig Little
got tired
of riding
in the car,
so he turned
into
an airplane
by rolling down
the window
and letting
his hands
be wings.

Donuts

On the way home
Pig Little's mom
bought donuts.
Pig Little
liked donuts.
But better than donuts
he loved the holes
in the center.
But to eat the hole
he had to eat
the donut too.
So he did.

Home

When Pig Little
got home
he found
that the beach
had come home
with him.
All his treasures
filled up
his night table,
and when he took off
his bathing suit,
his arms
were still warm
from the sun.
And when he took off
his cap,
he found
enough sand on the floor
to make
a small
hill.

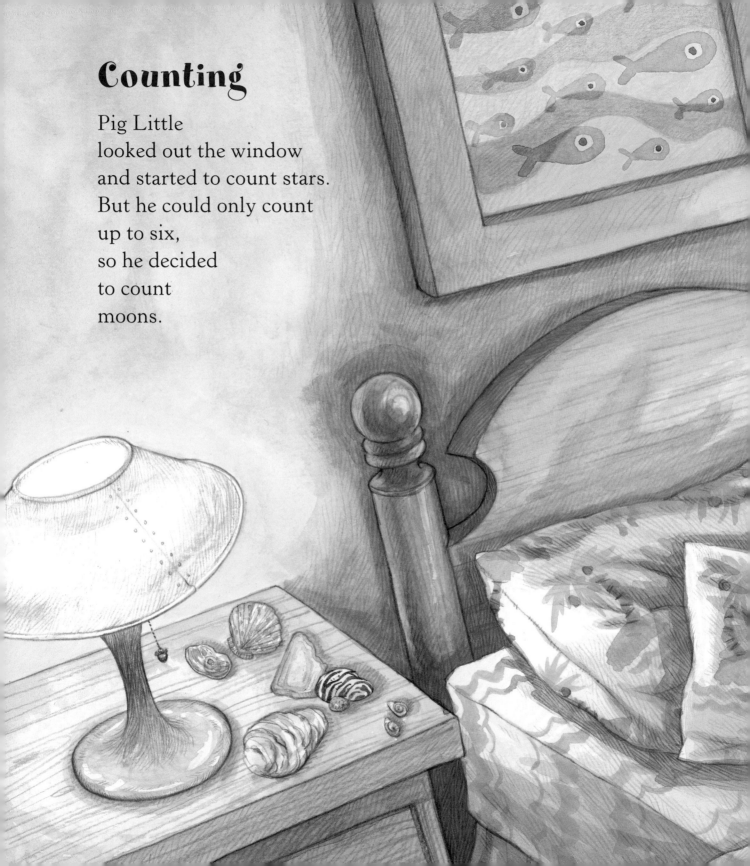

Counting

Pig Little
looked out the window
and started to count stars.
But he could only count
up to six,
so he decided
to count
moons.

Star Sailor

Pig Little's bed
was a blue-blanket sea.
He could make
giant waves
by just raising
one knee.
But when
his battleship sounded
the big-wave alarm,
he'd lower his knee,
and the sea
would be
calm.
So Pig Little
weighed the anchors
of his eyes,
and between
starfish and stars
he set sail
on a sea
of
dreams.